Bantam Books in the Choose Your Own Adventure® Series
Ask your bookseller for the books you have missed

Choose Your Own Adventure Books for young readers

WAR WITH THE EVIL POWER MASTER

BY R.A. MONTGOMERY

ILLUSTRATED BY PAUL ABRAMS

BANTAM BOOKS
TORONTO • NEW YORK • LONDON • SYDNEY • AUCKLAND

RL 5, IL age 10 and up

WAR WITH THE EVIL POWER MASTER
A Bantam Book / October 1984

CHOOSE YOUR OWN ADVENTURE is a registered trademark of
Bantam Books, Inc. Registered in U.S. Patent and Trademark
Office and elsewhere.

Original conception of Edward Packard

Front cover art by Ralph Reese.

ISBN 0-553-24523-6

Published simultaneously in the United States and Canada

Bantam Books are published by Bantam Books, Inc. Its trade-
mark, consisting of the words "Bantam Books" and the por-
trayal of a rooster, is Registered in U.S. Patent and Trademark
Office and in other countries. Marca Registrada. Bantam
Books, Inc. 666 Fifth Avenue, New York, New York 10103.

PRINTED IN THE UNITED STATES OF AMERICA

O   0 9 8 7 6 5 4 3 2

To Ramsey and Anson

WARNING!!!

Do not read this book straight through from beginning to end! These pages contain many different adventures you may have as you track down the Evil Power Master. From time to time as you read along, you will be asked to make a choice. Your choice may lead to success or disaster.

The adventures you take are a result of your choice. You are responsible because you choose! After you make your choice, follow the instructions to see what happens to you next.

Think carefully before you make a decision. Danger lurks at every turn. One move could lead you straight into the clutches of the Evil Power Master . . . or it could help you save the universe.

Good luck!

"The Evil Power Master is back, Flppto," you shout angrily to your Martian friend. "He's at it again!"

"Calm down, calm down, Commander. Now, tell me what's happening. Slowly," Flppto says in his even tone.

Getting up from your desk, you hand Flppto a copy of the message that has just come in from a remote sector of the vast Lacoonian System. The news is grim:

SUDDEN TOTAL DESTRUCTION OF PLANETS HAEMOG AND AROUTH, SECTOR 31-47-89. EVIL POWER MASTER CLAIMS RESPONSIBILITY.

You are primary unit commander of the Lacoonian System Rapid Force—a position of enormous responsibility for a person of your age. A natural leader, you earned your rank through hard work, courage, and skill. Your colleague and teammate is Flppto, a Martian of great abilities. Together you must protect the system from attack by renegade planets and forces.

Turn to page 2.

The Lacoonian System is composed of several galaxies and thousands of planets. It is the most successful experiment in civilization for both life forms and artificial intelligence. For millennia it has provided stability and freedom for all its members.

A price has been paid for this freedom, though: it has provoked the anger and envy of those planets denied membership in the System. Some were rejected because they were dying civilizations, failed experiments in life. Still other planets were excluded because the Lacoonian Congress felt they had greater potential for evil than for good. These evil planets have banded together under the leadership of a negative life force who calls himself the Evil Power Master. They are the renegades against whom you and Flppto struggle. They are dedicated to the destruction of the Lacoonian system.

Flppto looks up from the message in his hand. The Martian's usual self-control is replaced by anger. He crumples the paper in his fist.

"Did you expect anything else, Commander? We both knew that the Evil Power Master would be back. We are sadly familiar with his magical powers—or what some call magical powers. Here one minute, there the next. A beam of destructive light today, a cloud of poison gas tomorrow. A corrupt government official in a high position, a feeling of dread that cloaks a city, or a shower of missiles on the mother planet, Lacoos."

Go on to the next page.

"You're right, Flppto. I hoped we had destroyed him in the Purple Days War, which took so many lives in such a short time. I hoped, Flppto; you did, too."

Flppto nods in agreement and speaks again.

"Well, Commander, don't be hard on yourself. You did your best. Right now he is back in full force, seeking revenge for the renegade planets we've destroyed. His power must be strong again, or he would never have attacked. What form he will take this time remains to be seen."

"But what should we do, Flppto? We can't just sit and wait. We could go right to Sector 31-47-89 and check it out, but that means calling in the space vehicle from patrol. Or we could call in all unit commanders and meet with the Lacoonian Congress to plan for defense and attack."

If you decide to check out Sector 31-47-89 immediately, turn to page 6.

If you decide to call in unit commanders for a meeting with the Congress, turn to page 8.

"Look at this, Tara! It's a plan and timetable for takeover after the Congress gives in."

UNIT 3: OCCUPY GREAT HALL. UNIT 2B: OCCUPY COMPUTER CONTROL CENTER. UNIT 1: DISARM RAPID FORCE. UNIT 5: CONTROL INFORMATION CENTER. UNIT 4: CONTROL FOOD DISTRIBUTION.

"They're so confident of success! Let's do a check with the Central Computer Service and run down the other terminals. That should give us the location of other bases."

Tara hesitates.

"What's up, Tara?" you ask.

"Whoever was here might come back. These people aren't stupid. Let's wait here and try to capture one of them."

You consider this. "But on the other hand," you say, "time is of the essence. The Evil Power Master is as good as his word. He'll destroy those planets unless we can get to him. We must deactivate the laser cannon, or whatever he's using."

If you decide to wait where you are on the chance that someone will return, turn to page 46.

If you decide to check the Central Computer Service in hopes of locating the other bases and the main headquarters of the Evil Power Master, turn to page 49.

"Okay! You've got us. Don't hurt her."

You relinquish your creature and walk toward the other one, trying desperately to come up with a plan to save Tara and yourself—and the Lacoonian System.

There is a slight movement behind the creature. Suddenly you realize it's Flppto sneaking up, laser blaster at the ready.

Flppto fires. The creature drops to the floor. Flppto fires again, and the second creature falls.

"Flppto, how did you get here?" you shout.

"Simple, Earthling. I know your hunches well. And I also know that you usually need help. So here I am."

At that moment there is a rumbling sound and a shaking of the floor. The building is falling apart! Then a metallic voice pierces the air.

"FOOLS! YOU WILL NEVER DEFEAT ME."

These are the last words you'll ever hear.

The End

6

"Let's go out there and have a look, Flppto. We'll see what he's up to this time, or at least get some clues as to what to expect next."

Flppto nods. But before you can leave, it is essential to inform headquarters of your intention. Your destination is a remote sector of the galaxy closest to the edge of the Void of Niro—a void so large that travel in the zone can be perilous. The last time you were there, you barely got out! Flppto communicates with headquarters. His rapid and logical Martian mind lets him convey the message quickly.

"Ready, Flppto?"

"Of course," he responds.

You and Flppto move to the teletransporter for immediate dematerialization and thought-speed travel.

Twenty-seven minutes later you begin to rematerialize aboard the space frigate *Menton*. The ship's commander is Sartan, a highly respected combat leader and orbit station commander. She is waiting by the teletransporter to welcome you.

"Hello, Sartan," you say as you rematerialize completely. "My body needs some minor adjustments—the parts don't seem to fit together."

"Welcome, Commander. Perhaps one of the crew can help."

"No, thanks." You wiggle around a bit. "There it is. I've got it now. Good!"

Turn to page 11.

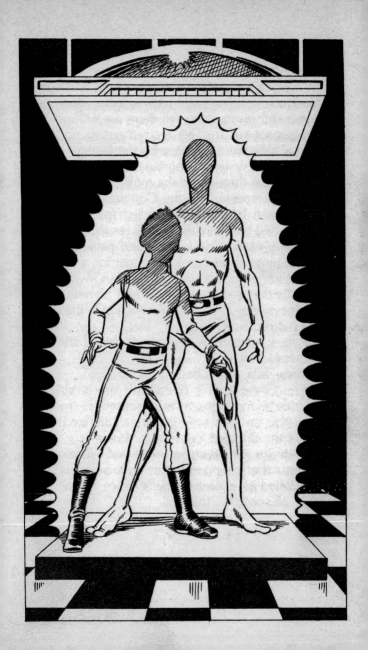

"Flppto, prepare a message to all unit commanders, ordering them back to base. Alert base command on Lacoos. Tell them we will make a hyperspace return. This is a red emergency!"

You are greeted at base by the leaders of the Lacoonian System Congress, elected representatives from throughout the multigalactic system. The spokesperson for the Congress is Tara, an old woman from one of the first space colonies established by Earthlings. She is respected for her firmness, wisdom, judgment, and patience. Tara is also remembered as a fierce warrior, a heroine of the early days of the Purple Days War, when bandits ravaged the independent planets. Now she faces you. There is determination in the set of her mouth.

"So, Commander, it's our old friend the Evil Power Master, is it?"

"Yes, Tara. He is back."

The Great Hall is filled with the babble of countless languages, as representatives from all over the multigalactic universe talk excitedly about the dreaded Evil Power Master.

With the swiftness of a forest that falls silent at an intruder's appearance, the noise is extinguished as a deep, metallic voice fills all corners, all spaces of the Hall.

Go on to the next page.

"GIVE UP, FOOLS. YOUR TIME HAS COME. YOU HAVE WITNESSED MY POWER IN THE PAST. HAEMOG AND AROUTH ARE JUST RE- MINDERS.

"SUBMIT TO MY WILL, OR EARTH, MAR- ZINA, AND ONE MORE PLANET OF MY CHOOSING WILL DISAPPEAR.

"YOU HAVE JUST THREE DAYS TO GIVE ME YOUR ANSWER."

You turn to Tara, who sits quietly, hands folded in her lap, eyes half-shut in meditation.

"Well, Tara, what do you think?"

"There is no time to think, Commander. There is only time to act."

You know that she is right. Marzina has a popu- lation 723 times the size of Earth's. Such large- scale destruction of life is unthinkable. Suddenly you have an idea. "Tara—that voice. I've heard it before. I've always believed the Evil Power Mas- ter has a base here on Lacoos. When he's in human form, it's natural for him to be right here. I believe I know where the voice is coming from. Let me chase it down."

She nods her head.

"Yes, I've thought before that the enemy could be among us. Would you like me to work with you, or will you pursue him on your own for now?"

If you decide to go this mission alone, turn to page 18.

If you decide to join forces with Tara, turn to page 15.

Your plan involves a visit to this remote sea farm on the western coast of the main island of Lacoos. There on the sea farm, hundred-foot-long fish were once raised and harvested as food. For many years, aquaculture has been passed over in favor of new and more profitable food sources. But you recall that a small group has remained on at Pwasonn to conduct special experiments.

You must decide how to approach Pwasonn. You could pretend to be a marine biologist from a remote planet in the Lacoonian System, researching aquaculture for your planet's food needs.

Or you could approach the Pwasonn Facility by stealth, and monitor what is going on with electronic optical and audio gear.

If you choose to pretend you are an interested marine biologist, turn to page 12.

If you choose stealth, turn to page 23.

You follow Flppto and Sartan into the command room, where a three-dimensional model of the galactic sector is displayed by laser.

Sartan points to the model of the sector.

"So there you see it. Or, rather, you *don't* see it. Haemog and Arouth were in their usual orbital paths, then they weren't. Their destruction was complete. All that remained in their place was a murmur of anguish, which we picked up on the sound recorder."

Sartan keys the recorder, and a haunting sound fills the room. As you stare thoughtfully at the map, an idea pops into your head.

"What about light? Did you pick up any light radiation, Sartan?"

"Of course, Commander. One trail of light seems to lead toward the Void; another heads off toward the planet Follop."

You look up at Flppto, who has followed your train of thought. He has already planned the routes the two of you can take. Route one leads to Follop, route two to the Void of Niro.

You and Flppto confer quickly and decide on your destination. Sartan offers to supply you with equipment, a vehicle, and a droid or two to assist you on your mission. In minutes you are ready to depart.

If you choose to go to the Void of Niro, turn to page 16.

If you choose to go to Follop, turn to page 21.

The Rapid Force headquarters has a locker room where crew members keep civilian clothes for off-duty times. You slip out of the Great Hall unnoticed and hurry to the locker room. No one is there. Good! You take off your unit commander uniform, storing it carefully in a locker, and don a simple, anonymous, blue-green jumpsuit.

Outside you locate a transporter, sign for it at the guard desk, and take off for the remote Pwasonn Facility. It takes you most of the day to get there. The sea farm is isolated, quiet, undisturbed—a backwater in the busy worlds of the Lacoonian System. When you arrive, the suns are in their passing mode, and the briny water reflects their rays in a brilliant shimmer of color. Out on a dock are two people hauling in nets.

Walking up to them as casually as you can, you ask, "Can I give you a hand?"

"Sure. We can always use help—we're short-handed out here these days," says a middle-aged man with sunburned face and arms, and a pepper-and-salt beard. "What brings you out to Pwasonn? We don't get many visitors."

"I'm a marine biologist from the planet Vito, out in Sector 36-43-28. My lab chief asked me to zip over here and ask your people how you get those fish to grow so big. Do you mind if I take a look around?"

Go on to the next page.

"Help yourself. But I'll tell you—it's nearly suppertime. Why don't you have a meal with us? Tomorrow you can get to work. My name is Marc, by the way."

"Thanks, Marc," you reply. "Sounds like a good plan."

Later that evening you are sitting at dinner with Marc and two others, Louise and Jose. They seem friendly and open. Maybe your instincts were wrong this time. These people don't seem to be hiding anything. They seem normal.

Just as you are about to leave the table to turn in, the loudspeaker over the entranceway blurts out, "Reports coming in. Repeat, reports now coming in."

Marc jumps up from his chair. There is a harsh look on his face.

"I'll go. You stay here," he snaps.

Jose and Louise seem to come to attention. Then Marc is gone.

There was something in the message, something in Marc's tone, the sudden tension in the air that you know means trouble.

If you try to leave the room with the excuse that you are tired, turn to page 42.

If you decide it's best to stay as close to Jose and Louise as you can and await Marc's return, turn to page 75.

"Tara, I will be honored if you join me. The Evil Power Master defies ordinary approaches. Your experience is needed. Thank you."

"Tut, tut! Think nothing of it. Now let's leave this dreary hall and its babbling. I can hardly hear myself think."

Once away, you explain to Tara that the voice reminded you somewhat of a recording made by a terrorist group, years back. The recording had been a demand for money.

"Remember the Purple Days War and the terrorist gang that tried to blackmail the Congress for three hundred million Lacoonian dollars, Tara?"

"Who could forget? They almost succeeded when they hijacked that giant intergalactic transport," says Tara.

"Well, I think it could be the same gang. I remember where their headquarters was located. Let's start there."

The major city of Lacoos is strung out along both sides of the river Klingda. Towers and spheres as tall as forty stories are spanned by graceful arches serving as walkways.

You and Tara approach one of the large spheres on the far side of the city, overlooking the river. Years ago the top floor had been the headquarters for the terrorist gang. It's just a hunch on your part that the gang may be at it again, but you have followed hunches before, and they have usually been right.

Turn to page 20.

16

"The Void it is, Flppto. We've done it before. No time to waste—that light track will vanish before too long."

Flppto does not respond; he is too busy with additional calculations. You let him be.

Sartan has ordered her crew of droids to prepare a high-speed space vehicle for the dash into the Void. She leads you to it for a quick inspection. One of the droids is shaped like a bullet, with two sets of armlike elements. It stands by to load and fire the vessel into the Void. The droid communicates in rapid-fire, humanoid speech.

"Allsetandreadytogopowerplantpositivethree andantishockshieldsinplace."

"Hey, Sartan, this ship is great. It's an old model, but a good one. I flew this kind back in the Purple Days War."

While you finish inspecting the space vehicle, Flppto completes his calculations. Then he speaks.

Go on to the next page.

"I have disturbing news. The light track intensifies near the center of the Void. This has never happened before!"

"What are you trying to tell us, Flppto? Do you want us to cancel?"

"I want nothing, Commander. We Martians are fortunately above wanting—we think, we act, we want not."

"I get it. You are recommending that we split up. It's your great love of being on your own, right?"

He nods.

"It would be wisest to come into the light zone from three different directions. Safer, too, I might add," says Flppto. Turning to Sartan, he asks, "Your droid will accompany us?"

Sartan nods her agreement.

If you go along with Flppto's suggestion to split up, turn to page 24.

If you override Flppto's suggestion, turn to page 29.

"Alone for now, Tara. I think your talents are needed here on Lacoos. And I feel the need to pursue this on my own. I won't even take Flp-pto."

She nods.

"Go with peace and goodness. You will triumph. I believe it."

While the other commanders and members of Congress take their seats in the Great Hall to discuss the Evil Power Master's threat, you slip out unnoticed through a side entrance. In the warmth of the afternoon suns, it seems impossible that so much is wrong in the universe.

The voice of the Evil Power Master, the metallic twang, has jarred an odd and startling memory from the past. Many years ago, you listened in on an experiment recording fish sounds at the Pwasonn Research Facility. Now that far-off day has come back to you—how you sat with earphones on, listening to the conversations of two giant fish. Pwasonn Facility has been almost ignored for the last decade. Maybe, just maybe, it is a base for the Evil Power Master.

Turn to page 10.

No one is outside the sphere; all seems quiet. Access is simple: no questions, no guards, no hassle. You take the shuttle stairway to the top level of the sphere. Using a digital lock pick—standard issue to the Rapid Force—you enter the space once occupied by the terrorists. The room seems deserted except for an old computer console and display unit in a corner. A green glow bathes the display unit.

Moving across the room, you find a short message on the computer screen:

FOOLS: YOUR TIME IS ALMOST UP. CAPITULATE NOW!

"We're on to them, Tara; it's got to be them. This is a message to the Congress. The deadline is too soon."

On a whim you hit the key on the computer for PRINT, and the old-fashioned daisy-wheel printer next to the console clacks dutifully away.

Turn to page 4.

The planet Follop is part of a star system of unique configuration. Triple moons and a giant sun occupy a remote galactic space. Life forms on Follop are non-humanoid, and considered dangerous to explorers. Space literature abounds with reports of crews that never returned from the planet, or survivors who were badly mauled.

Recently a humanoid colony was established on Follop, which is ideally situated for special types of agricultural study. Your cousin Colin is part of the Follop agricultural research team.

The journey to Follop is a harrowing hyperspace trip. After hours of dodging asteroids and comets, you are in orbit, preparing for a landing. But intense solar-flare eruptions have knocked out contact with the Follop base station. All methods of communication have been disrupted.

Flppto has been doing his best, but until now the results have been negative.

"Wait a minute, Commander. I'm getting something."

"What is it, Flppto?"

"An SOS. It's coming from a minor orbiting planet of Follop. It's off our flight plan. If we answer it, we delay our landing on Follop. What do you want to do?"

If you decide to answer the SOS,
turn to page 25.

If you decide to proceed with the landing on
Follop, to follow the light track and deal with
the SOS later, turn to page 33.

Pretending to be a marine biologist would be tricky—you know little of that specialty. Stealth it is, then. You borrow a transporter from the depot at Rapid Force headquarters. Pwasonn is a good distance away, and the journey must go unnoticed. You delay your departure until the next morning, so that you will arrive at dusk. Then, when darkness has fallen, you approach the Pwasonn Facility from the thickly wooded hillsides to the north. The moons, unfortunately for you, are high and unusually luminous. The light of the stars also beats back the night. You are a target—alone, unprotected—in the pale blue-black night. Every move you make threatens to reveal you to the life forms guarding the area. All is quiet, but a tremor of fear shakes you. It could be the force of evil that you feel, the dread that can freeze people in thought and action, allowing the Evil Power Master to take over. Dread is creeping over you like a chill.

If you back away from Pwasonn and the creeping feeling of dread, turn to page 30.

If you go on, ignoring the feeling, turn to page 39.

"Okay, Flppto, I'll follow your lead. How do we do it?"

He gestures for you and Sartan to wait while he performs additional logic sequences. The bullet-shaped droid slides noiselessly to Flppto's side, offering its computer storage banks to be tapped for necessary information.

"I've got it," Flppto says. "We will not use space vehicles. We will propel ourselves at one-second intervals with space-packs, allowing this droid here to lead the way. Just follow his path and split up at my signal."

It's a dangerous way to travel. You won't be dematerialized as in teletransport. You will have none of the protection of the space vehicle and its systems. But there is an advantage—you will be far less conspicuous. "After all, who knows what's out there?" you say to yourself.

"Okay, Flppto, I hope you're right."

Turn to page 27.

"It's the unwritten rule of space, Flppto. We cannot ignore a distress signal. This is a tough sector of the galaxy. In we go."

The bullet-shaped droid is eager for action and prepares your space vehicle for the landing. The droid has a name, but it is tough to spell and impossible to pronounce. So you call him Tonto, after a famous Earthling. Like the original Tonto, this droid is quiet, capable, and ready to help out in a jam. You and Flppto make expeditionary preparations, readying the radiation counters,the stun guns, the life-support packs, and the communicators.

With a swirl of dust, the capsule nestles down in a sandy area on this minor planet. The sky outside is a light green, the sand a darkish brown. Vegetation at the edge of the sand area is gigantic, tropical, and dense. It is a continuous mass of tangled green. Cactuslike plants dot the green with a pale blue-gray, topped by vermilion.

You key a transmit button, trying to answer the SOS call.

Turn to page 28.

You put on your space-packs, and moments later the bullet-shaped droid is propelled toward the light track. Flppto follows, then you.

Eighty seconds later, drifting in the darkness of the Void, you reach the light. Suddenly you are out of control! The light stream, cold and harsh, envelops you. A voice pierces your mind.

"WELCOME, COMMANDER. IT'S ABOUT TIME YOU JOINED US."

In the Void, the light has the force of a waterfall. You tumble in the rushing stream, buffeted by bursts of energy that leave painful bruises on your body. You fight to remain alive. You lose track of the others. Then the voice speaks again.

"IT IS USELESS, COMMANDER, TO STRUGGLE AGAINST ME. I, THE EVIL POWER MASTER, THE ULTIMATE POWER, AM INVINCIBLE. I HAVE AN OFFER FOR YOU. JOIN ME AND BE ONE OF MY CHOSEN LIEU-TENANTS. OTHERWISE . . . DEATH."

If you join the Evil Power Master, hoping it will gain you time, turn to page 36.

If you refuse, turn to page 91.

"This is Lacoonian System Rapid Force to SOS call, over."

A crackle emerges from your communicator. It intensifies. Then you hear a distant, weak voice.

"Help! Help . . . Mobile Agricultural Research Group Thirty-two. We are in the jungle. Saw you land. We've been attacked. Our energy is weakening. Haven't much time left. Help!"

"It could be a trap, Commander," says Flppto. "This SOS may be a decoy, to lure us away from our mission. I think we should analyze the message."

"But is there time, Flppto? Can we take the chance, and risk their lives?"

If you decide to wait and analyze the tape of the message, turn to page 55.

If you decide to go in right now, turn to page 52.

"Sorry, Flppto, but we're playing it safe. We'll all go in the space vehicle."

"You Earthlings will never learn. Oh well, I've tried—the gods know I've tried."

The vehicle is armed only with sound-and-light stun weapons. You reject the nuclear devastators. "They're too final," you think. You, Flppto, and the droid climb aboard the vehicle.

"Systems set. Course planned. Air locks secured. Fire!" says Sartan.

The extraordinary acceleration forces you back into your body-mold command chair. The G-gauge on the forward control column rapidly moves to 5; then 6; then 7, and beyond. It's almost too much. But the ride into the Void is smooth. There are no obstacles, and the constant temperature is a stunning minus 460 degrees.

"Hey! What's that?" asks Flppto.

Turn to page 32.

The feeling of dread almost paralyzes you. You start to retreat slowly at first. Finally you run for your life, fear trailing you like streamers.

Up one hill, across a flat stretch, then up a final, steeper hill. You throw yourself to the ground and gasp for breath. Then you peer over the rim of the hill at the research facility below.

A multicolored light source throbs near the main building. Fascinated, you watch as the light intensifies. A cloud of purple smoke billows into the air, and out of the bottom of the cloud steps a life form. It's hard to make out the shape, but it looks as if there are three heads attached to a normal body.

Suddenly you *know*. "It's him—the Evil Power Master in life form!" you say aloud, almost shouting. "I've found his base!"

You reach desperately for your communicator. Clicking it on, you whisper to Tara your location; then you describe what is taking place before you. A band of followers bows before the Evil Power Master as he begins to move toward the building. The lights turn to a lurid green.

Every muscle is tense as you wait for Tara to act. And act she does. The rage seeps out of you as patrol craft and galactic fighters swarm the area.

Watching with distaste as his followers try to flee, the Evil Power Master stands alone. He is encircled by a heavily armed team of Rapid Force members. As he is captured, you see a smirk on his lips. But—for now—the Lacoonian System is safe.

The End

"What's what, Flppto?"

Then you see it. A bright green flash off the port side of the capsule. The bullet-shaped droid has already zeroed in on it with its sensing analyzers and is issuing a report.

"Brightgreenlightlifegeneratedreflectingofflife mademassofdeepdensity."

"Got it. But talk more slowly next time, will you?"

"Ican't."

Suddenly you are in orbit around a hexagonal green object. It is about the size of one of Jupiter's moons. Along one side are what appear to be portholes and a complex set of hangar doors and space moats. The green light flashes again and again. No life forms are visible.

If you decide to try for a landing on the porthole side, turn to page 48.

If you decide to reconnoiter the area, turn to page 60.

"The primary mission, our primary mission, is to close in on the Evil Power Master," you say.

"But, Commander, it's the code of space to answer an SOS."

"I know, Flppto, but I am overriding tradition or laws or whatever you call it. Our mission is more important, much more important than one crew in trouble. We must save millions of lives. The Evil Power Master threatens planets all over the universe."

"It is your choice, Commander, and your responsibility. Please make a recording of my formal objection to your decision."

"As you wish, Flppto, but I won't change my mind. We won't ignore them. But our first and most important mission is to track down the Evil Power Master. We might be on a wild-goose chase, searching for a light track leading to Follop, but I stick by my decision."

Flppto nods. You see the look of concern on his face. But you are convinced that you are right.

The space vehicle is in position over Follop, and you give the order to descend to the planet's surface. Slowly the ship moves into Follop's atmosphere. Outside there is the usual red glow from reentry friction. Then, with a soft bounce of its retrorockets to cushion the landing, the ship is down.

Go on to the next page.

"Wow! Flppto, look at that!"

Outside the thick, protective portals you glimpse what must once have been a thriving, industrious, and elegant space colony. The city, or what's left of it, smolders in the bright light of the system's suns. Fires here and there nibble at the

vestiges of buildings. No life forms are in evidence.

Turn to page 38.

"Okay, okay. I'll join. But what then, Evil Power Master? What then?" you ask, suddenly released from the buffeting of the energy in the light stream.

"Riches beyond belief, my new friend, beyond your ability to imagine."

Moments later you are resting in a globe fashioned of the clearest glass. In the globe with you are three people—an old man, a youth, and a middle-aged woman. There is something about their expression that makes you uneasy. Their faces have an unfinished look. Their eyes, as they stare at you with the utmost concentration, seem to be missing something. The youth speaks.

"Wasn't hard, was it? I mean, joining up with us."

You nod in agreement, feeling a rush of power, knowing that you have made a bargain with evil.

The End

"Flppto, I just don't know. This sounds fishy to me. Why should the SOS come from Colin? Too much of a coincidence. The Evil Power Master is capable of mind reading. He could have picked up brain waves about my cousin. I think it's too . . ."

But you never finish your sentence. A beam of energy destroys your ship. All that remains is a cloud of purple dust.

The End

"From the looks of this, we are too late to help."

"Commander, this is not the trademark of the Evil Power Master. This is conventional destruction. This is everyday, war-torn mess. Looks more like the work of the Narras, or their equally vicious enemies, the Booduns."

You nod in agreement, but something still nags at you.

"How about the light track that we were supposed to be following?"

"Whatever it was, Commander, it has no meaning for us now. There is nothing left; we came too late," Flppto says with resignation.

"Flppto—we can't know that for sure unless we investigate. The light *must* have meant something. This may be the work of the Evil Power Master after all. And there may be survivors."

"One thing we do know, Commander—those people who issued the SOS still need our help. What is our next step?"

If you decide to get out of your ship and search for survivors, turn to page 61.

If you decide to leave Follop, to search for those who sent the SOS, turn to page 43.

Dread or no dread, you know you must go on with the mission. You make it beyond the first perimeter warning zone. The wire fences, a relic of the past, give way easily to your laser cutters. No alarm is sounded. A series of ditches, almost moats, surround the main building. They are filled with slimy, green water. You find a log—old and rotting, but sturdy enough, you hope. Laying it across the first ditch, you inch your way over the oozing slime.

Now you are in place behind a stand of short red pines. Their resinous smell fills the air and mingles with the salt of the sea—almost an Earth smell. You take a deep breath.

Now the long wait begins—the waiting and the watching. You set up the optical gear that you have lugged so carefully over difficult terrain. Next, you hook up the sound equipment. At the main building all is quiet. A single light burns in the front room. You focus the scanner on the large floor-to-ceiling windows.

Go on to the next page.

Through the scope you see three people seated around a table. Two are your age. Well dressed. Ordinary looking. Smiling. The third is an older, stern-looking man in rumpled clothes. They are studying a multigalactic map of the Lacoonian System. You switch on the audio equipment.

"Ha! We've got them running, don't we?" The older man rubs his hands together. "The Laconians will give up this time. We'll explode those planets with the laser cannon. The universe is ours. All ours!"

Turn to page 44.

"Well, I'm exhausted," you say. "That's it for me. Good night, and thanks for letting me join your group. I'm learning a lot."

A quick glance passes between Jose and Louise. Louise looks furtively toward the door where Marc left the room. Jose speaks.

"Good idea," he says heartily. "I'll show you to your room. Can't be too careful out here. Strange things have been known to happen at night."

Moments later you are in a small, cell-like room staring at four whitewashed concrete walls. You wait for Jose's footsteps to recede.

It's all quiet now. Two large, old, sodium-vapor lamps illuminate the compound where the tanks house the giant fish. It looks safe, but . . . What did Jose mean about strange things happening in the night? you ask yourself.

If you decide to investigate where Marc went and what he's up to, turn to page 79.

If you decide it's time for help, use your communicator and get Flppto here fast. Turn to page 82.

"Okay, Flppto—we're answering the SOS. There just isn't much we can do here."

With heavy hearts you turn from the Follop colony and leave this once lovely place, on the track of the SOS. The senders might have a clue to what happened on Follop.

"Nearing transmission zone of the SOS, Commander. Hover or go in?" asks Flppto hours later.

"We'll go on in. Prepare ship for landing. Observe all emergency procedures for hostile action. Lock and load stun equipment."

Turn to page 74.

44

You've heard enough. This is it. Just three people with a laser cannon. You calculate that they are probably using satellites as redirectional shields to deflect shots to remote planets. How they amplify the laser is a mystery. But the people are *real; live,* you think.

Just then, without warning, they change form before your eyes. They merge first into crystal shapes, then change into vivid green lights.

A shock goes through you as you realize that you have found the Evil Power Master. This is his base. You are frustrated—you have no power to capture him. Quickly, you radio a report to Tara and await her next move. All you can do is hope the wait won't be too long.

The End

"I'll stay with the computer, Tara."

"Fine. I'll talk with Congress," she says.

The computer team is superb. Their search procedures are brilliant, efficient, and—ultimately—productive.

"Pay dirt, Commander! Final trace going through in moments."

The woman who heads the computer team hands you a printout of the other remote terminal locations. You feel triumphant. The Evil Power Master has made an enormous mistake in using conventional computers.

"Thank you, Colonel. Well done."

You gaze down at the printout. It indicates eleven supplementary terminals, representing bases of the Evil Power Master. You feared this but were prepared for the worst. But one terminal is missing from the printout—the primary one!

"The primary source, Colonel. The primary source! Where is it?" you ask.

Turn to page 63.

"We'll wait here, Tara," you say.

The room is stifling hot. You begin to take notice of the profusion of tropical plants in the room. It's odd—you hadn't noticed them earlier. Bamboo, vines, palms. A veritable jungle occupies nearly half of the space.

A strange drowsiness overcomes you, and you slump down against the wall. Tara seems tired, too.

Slowly, from out of the jumbled mass of vegetation, a pair of creatures emerges. They look like a cross between a lizard and a sloth. With slow movements they approach the two of you.

One of the creatures moves to the computer and types in a message.

WE WILL NEUTRALIZE ENEMY. AWAITING YOUR COMMANDS, MASTER.

The other creature reaches out a long, scaly arm and exposes sharp, menacing talons. The creature gurgles, "Hail to the glorious Evil Power Master."

You reach up and grab his wrist, twisting the scaly arm with all your strength. Slowly you bear down, and the creature screams in pain. But the other creature has scuttled over to Tara and holds her in a firm grip. With its talons at Tara's throat, the creature speaks.

"Give up or I will kill her."

If you surrender, turn to page 5.

If you refuse to surrender, turn to page 77.

"Let's go right on in. There's a time limit for us out here in the Void. This vehicle is too small to support life for more than six hours."

"Very good, Commander," Flppto says.

The droid has positioned the vehicle for landing. You have second thoughts, but it is too late—or almost. One of the hangar doors is rolling open, revealing a pure white light. A chill spreads through you as the light penetrates the vehicle. It illuminates Flppto's face, which is grave with concern.

If you enter the hangar, turn to page 92.

If you put on full reverse, turn to page 94.

"Let's get back to headquarters and the Central Computer Service. That's our best lead. We can send a patrol to watch this place, Tara."

"Fine with me."

Before you can reach the shuttle stairs that lead to ground level, three orange-skinned creatures burst in. Each has a ring of eyes around its bulbous head. One of them cries out: "Freecg zircjys—myocardinium!"

Go on to the next page.

Dropping to a crouch, you grab your laser gun and fire. Zap!

Two of the creatures are stunned. The third leaps to the stairway and disappears down the steps.

It's no use following, you decide; that orange

creature was too fast. You and Tara race back to headquarters. Rushing to the Central Computer Service, you order an immediate trace on the computer.

Turn to page 54.

"Flppto, let's go. Someone needs help." You reach for the door just as a white, blinding explosion rocks the vehicle. The droid is hurled to the floor, its voice synthesizer damaged. It repeats, over and over, "It's a very nice day, it's a very nice day, I thank you, thank you, thank."

Flppto has been slammed to the floor, too, where he lies shaking—less from fear, you suspect, than from the force of the fall. You are in a heap yourself. You swim in and out of a sea of pain and warmth. The pain becomes so severe that you lose consciousness. When you come to, you hear the droid prattling on about the weather.

Flppto is recovering. "Commander, don't move. You're hurt badly. We'll help you."

Go on to the next page.

You lie there while the two of them gather their own strength and begin to move toward you. With a rush of pain you fall into a deep, black space.

Down
        down
             down
                  into
                       pain.

When you awaken, the first thing you notice is one pair of humanoid eyes and one set of droid sensors peering at you. Flppto speaks.

"Commander, you are seriously injured. Whom do you wish to appoint to command the mission? The droid, Tonto, knows the sector better than we. It is also in communication with Sartan and her forces."

If you appoint Tonto, turn to page 70.

If you appoint Flppto, turn to page 72.

"Right away, Commander, right away," the head of the Service says.

You confer with Tara. She suggests that one of you talk to the Congress and let them know what's going on, warning them not to capitulate. The other should return to the terrorists' head-quarters to keep an eye on the computer.

If you decide to be the one to talk with the Congress, turn to page 68.

If you decide to return to the computer, turn to page 45.

"Let's have a closer look at the tape, Flppto. We'll analyze the voice, get a voice print and a truth analysis, check it for humanoid or non-humanoid characteristics."

"Right away, Commander."

"Get Tonto to help you, Flppto. That droid can produce amazing results."

"Right."

You sit tight, waiting for the analysis. A faked message luring a spaceship into dangerous areas is an old trick. Your primary mission is to track, expose, and eliminate the Evil Power Master. You are nervous that you have made a mistake by answering the SOS.

But before the analysis can be completed, the message is repeated with even greater urgency. This time it's signed "Colin." That's your cousin's name.

You must go. No one, no thing could have known that your cousin Colin was on the planet. Or could they? You shiver. The Evil Power Master has amazing powers.

If you want further identification, turn to page 37.

If you are satisfied that it is Colin, turn to page 57.

"That must be Colin. We're going in, Flppto. We'll leave the droid behind."

Flppto monitors the gas content of the enveloping atmosphere. It is breathable for you and the Martian. He opens the double air lock.

You step out onto the powdery brown sand. The place is hot and tropical. Bulbous storm clouds hover in the distance. Lightning flashes, swiftly followed by large, dark-blue raindrops. Moments later you cross the circle of sand and stand in the tangled mass of jungle vegetation.

"We'll use the machetes, Flppto."

But before the first slash of the machete is even completed, a scaly green vine encircles Flppto's arm. Other vines reach out, imprisoning your arms and legs.

At that moment a hairy beast—looking more like a bird than an ape—roars with anger. It stands before you, jaws snapping, then lunges toward you.

The vine that holds Flppto seems to cringe. Loosening its anacondalike grip, it retreats quickly into the greenery.

"Watch it, Flppto! That bird-ape is moving."

"I'll radio the droid."

"No time. We're sunk."

Just then there is a sharp, crashing sound, and the bird-ape tumbles forward, hitting the soft ground. Its huge beak quivers; its eyes rotate in astonishment.

Turn to page 62.

You decide not to use your weapons—yet.

Suddenly you hear a familiar voice. "Welcome. It's been too long. Yes, too long since we last met. You have changed."

Before your eyes appears the fabled Rendoxoll—the quintessence of artificial intelligence, and a hero of the Lacoonian system. You worked with Rendoxoll long ago. You have always admired its brilliance and dedication to the cause of Lacoonian freedom. But for years Lacoonians have believed Rendoxoll was destroyed in the Purple Days War.

Happy and confused, you ask, "But . . . but . . . how did you get here? Where are we, anyway?"

Rendoxoll swivels a full 360 degrees and waves its flipperlike mechanical arms. It speaks.

"When it became apparent to me several years ago that the Evil Power Master would not be stopped by mere human tactics, I removed myself to this remote and isolated sector to wait, and wait, and wait. Of course, I established a powerful force field."

You look at this marvel of self-created artificial intelligence from the planet F32. One thing is certain—Rendoxoll is always two swivels ahead. It suddenly dawns on you that your droid recognized Rendoxoll and was delighted to join it.

"Wait for what, Rendoxoll?"

Go on to the next page.

"For the Evil Power Master to make a mistake, Earthling. Use that jumbled mass of gray jelly you call a brain. The Evil Power Master was bound to slip up. I wanted to be sure that when he did, I'd be there."

You stare at Rendoxoll—this collection of circuits, bubble chambers, and storage banks—for several moments.

"What now?" you ask.

"Earthlings are always full of questions—how tiresome. But I will tell you. It is quite simple really. I just waited until the Evil Power Master changed into human form. He does that every so often, to get a real feeling for the people he is about to destroy. He has assumed the form of a young man and mingled with the crowd on Follop. We have to capture him. Would you like to lead my droids on the mission? It's dangerous, of course. But you are known for your bravery."

Pleased by Rendoxoll's praise, and ready for the challenge, you agree to do it. With a mixture of fear and excitement, you and the droids travel to Follop. Rendoxoll has provided you with special eyeglasses. When you get to Follop, you put them on, as instructed. Sure enough, the Evil Power Master is there. He has taken the form of a young man. But you can identify him by his strange, black aura, visible through the special glasses.

The droids position themselves strategically around the youth. They await your command. "Now!" you shout.

Turn to page 66.

"Too dangerous to do a direct approach. Let's take our time—nice and slow and careful. Prepare computer autopilot for search pattern."

"Yes, Commander. All set."

The capsule begins its zigzag pattern around the enormous green hexagon. The far side appears totally smooth, with no seams, no portholes, no anything. It's as green as a field in the spring.

Time passes. You look at the clock, startled to realize that you have been circling this strange space object for three hours.

Suddenly a swarm of delta wings—hyperspace fighting craft—streak out of the hangar doors and converge on your capsule with alarming precision. You can't see who is at the controls of these craft—the pilots' compartments have darkly shaded glass.

Flppto looks up from the command console.

"They're keyed into our evasive pattern, Commander. What shall we do?"

If you decide to use maximum destructive force, turn to page 95.

If you decide to wait and see what happens, turn to page 98.

"Come on, let's see what really happened here. Follow me," you command the others. You leave the protection of the ship.

Hours later, after you have searched through the devastated city, the only living creature you come across is an aged farmer. He is an exile from another colony. Condemned for a forgotten crime, he was sent to work the grain fields of Follop for life.

The farmer tells you that it was indeed the forces of the Evil Power Master who struck.

"Don't trust them, ever. They'll use anything they can to win. Here they used fire—simple fire—to destroy."

"What does the Evil Power Master want? Why?"

The old man looks at you grimly and speaks.

"Come now, that's easy enough. Power. Raw power. You're too late; he's gone. You'll never defeat him!"

Turn to page 65.

From out of the jungle steps Colin. In his hand is an ancient relic of Earth civilization—a rifle. He smiles and moves toward you.

"Colin! I thought we were supposed to be saving *you.*"

Colin smiles and greets you. Then he shows the weapon in his hand with some pride.

"It's an old zoologist's tool—it fires a tranquilizer. That creature will be fine in five or ten minutes. But let's get out of here before it wakes up. They can be nasty when provoked."

Colin points back to the jungle from which he had emerged, shaking his head sorrowfully.

"We were a team of eleven; three have survived. Our space pod is inactive, and we are unarmed."

"Who do you think is doing this? And why?" you ask.

"I think this could be one of the Evil Power Master's bases," Colin answers. "It's isolated. The vegetation provides great camouflage. And I just have a feeling, a strong feeling."

You nod and consider Colin's idea. What should you do next?

If you spend more time searching here, you might lose the trail of the Evil Power Master in space. On the other hand, this could be a good place to start the search. It is close to Follop and the mysterious light track.

If you want to stay where you are and search, turn to page 117.

If you want to go on to Follop, turn to page 67.

"One moment, Commander." The colonel scans the additional printouts, a look of misgiving on her face. You pace the small, cramped area of the computer center. Flppto sits calmly, gazing at the printout. Occasionally his eyes stray to the multigalactic map and the time indicator over the main computer.

"It's here, Commander. I've got it—the central computer terminal," the colonel says.

The center of the Evil Power Master's activity seems to be a nearby satellite. Further search, however, reveals that communication control appears to come from the planet Follop, far away on the edge of the Void of Niro. You know that in recent days communication with Follop has been almost impossible. You are on to something—you're convinced of it.

"Let's get out there, Flppto. There's no time to lose."

"Careful, Commander. Don't rush. Think it through. Let's talk with the Congress first."

"Martians!" you say. "Always so cautious. But you may have a point. . . ."

If you take Flppto's advice and talk with the Congress, turn to page 86.

If you follow your instinct and blast off with Flppto to Follop, turn to page 89.

You say goodbye to the farmer, return to base headquarters at Lacoos, and report in. There is a message awaiting you from the Evil Power Master. It reads:

FOOLISH HUMAN. YOU THINK YOU CAN DEAL WITH ME: THEN TRY. I CHALLENGE YOU TO A DUEL. MEET ME IN THE STADIUM OF AXUM AT NOON TOMORROW.
EVIL POWER MASTER

You have to agree to the challenge; this wanton destruction must stop! The next day finds you at the Stadium. The Evil Power Master has broadcast the news of the duel, and crowds overflow the stadium. You arrive not full of hope, but feeling that you are a sacrifice to evil.

In the center of the stadium, clad in the clothes of a simple peasant, stands the Evil Power Master. He is unarmed. He looks at you coolly, then throws his arms up to the sky. A horrible laugh spreads through the air.

"Fools! I'm too much for you." With a clap of thunder and a cloud of dust, the Evil Power Master disappears. You stand alone in the center of the stadium. You are relieved to be alive, but angry—his seeming cowardice has robbed you of the chance to do battle. "Next time," you think. "Next time."

The End

"Now!" they respond. They join artificial hands to form a solid ring around the youth. The Evil Power Master screams, and you give the order for the droids to immobilize him with a simple electrical current. With an unearthly shriek, the villain falls. He is yours!

Victorious, you take him back to Rendoxoll's base. Amid cheers and congratulations, the Evil Power Master is suspended in a gravity-free chamber. You hope the chamber will be his eternal home.

The End

You never have a chance to leave for Follop. The bird-ape that Colin felled in the jungle has roused itself and its fellow creatures for revenge. They surround your spacecraft. Slowly but surely, their sharp beaks and teeth penetrate its metal skin. Colin is a good shot, but his ancient rifle is inadequate. You flee the spaceship. Together with your crew and Colin, you are marooned on this strange planet, left to survive as best you can.

The End

"I'll talk to the Congress, Tara."

She nods her agreement. You leave immediately for the Great Hall, where all is chaos. Delegates from all over the universe are babbling in frightened confusion.

You approach the main table where the venerable leaders of the Congress are gathered. "Please, let me speak to our representatives," you say. Eager for any direction or guidance, the leaders give you the floor.

"Friends, don't give in. Have courage, I beseech you. The Evil Power Master can be defeated."

A murmur of disbelief greets your words. As you begin to speak again, the crowd jeers. Shouts of "Fool. . . ." "We've heard that speech before. . . ." "We'll all die!" resound throughout the Great Hall. You hold up your hands for silence, but no one listens.

Turn to page 73.

"You take over," you tell the droid. "You know the ship, the crew, and the sector we are in. I want you, however, to consult Flppto and Sartan on every move."

"Aye, aye, Commander. We'll carry on."

Turning slowly to face your Martian friend, you ask, "Flppto, tell me the truth. Exactly how badly am I hurt?"

There is a lengthy silence, and you are once again almost convulsed by waves of pain. Finally Flppto speaks.

"It's not good—not good at all, Commander. Broken femur of the left leg, smashed ulna and radius of the right arm, ruptured spleen, possible injuries to the kidneys, maybe the liver. Your blood pressure is bad, too."

Turn to page 76.

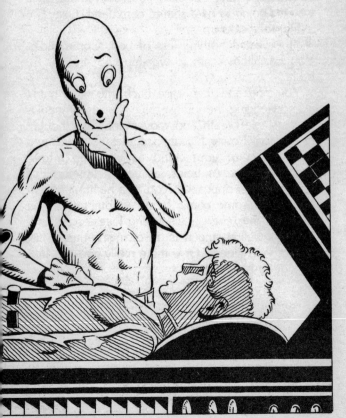

"Flppto, you're it. Sorry," you tell the droid, "but Flppto and I have been through a lot together. This is what has to be."

The droid nods in agreement. You are pleased to see that it takes the news well. It is the mark of a good leader.

"Don't forget, though, Tonto, I want Flppto to check everything out with you. Everything! In a way it's going to be a shared command. Okay?"

Flppto speaks up.

"I expected nothing less of you, Commander. You Earthlings seem to worship cooperation. So be it!"

You nod and then ease back into your bunk, acknowledging the intense pain that accompanies every single breath and movement. The thought of the Evil Power Master becomes confused and tangled up in your mind as you slip into a drugged sleep. At times, as you sleep, the Evil Power Master appears to you as a nightmarish figure out of some comic book. At other times he dissolves into energy, displaying love for the universe as well as anger. Is his changing nature just part of your illness? Or is there really another, better side to his nature?

Turn to page 100.

Then the voice—the metallic, twanging voice of the Evil Power Master—fills the room again.

"DON'T BE FOOLS. GIVE UP NOW! TIME IS RUNNING OUT. HESITATE AND YOU ARE DOOMED."

There is a momentary silence. Then the Great Hall fills with screams and shouts. The Congress has become a hysterical, frightened mob. The deadline is almost up. Doom is a few hours away.

Flppto rushes into the Great Hall. He has been in the computer room with Tara.

"Commander, I've got it! I know where the Evil Power Master is. He has a satellite orbiting this very planet. It's small, and its protection is limited. There are eleven similar satellites throughout the system—all under his control."

There is no time to think, only to act.

If you decide to launch an attack immediately, turn to page 114.

If you decide to inform Congress and get the members to order a full-scale attack, turn to page 83.

The landing goes smoothly, and you, Flppto, and the droid you brought from Sartan disembark into the breathable atmosphere. The droid performs a rapid computer-search of the immediate area: nothing.

The direction finder points to the last-known transmission site of the SOS. It leads toward an almost impenetrable jungle.

Flppto says, "Commander, I am uncomfortable. Something is not quite right."

You look questioningly at the droid. Its sensors indicate a life force in the area, but none of you sees any living creature.

"There must be a short circuit somewhere," you say.

The droid never has a chance to respond. There is a thundering, overwhelming snapping of giant jaws. You realize that your ship landed on top of an enormous creature. The grinning beast swallows the three of you in one gulp.

The End

"Thought I was tired, but I feel wide awake now. Is there any more coffee?"

Jose nods and fills your cup.

"How long have you been here at Pwasonn, Louise?" you ask.

"About a year," Louise answers.

You nod, stir some sugar into your cup, stare at the dark mixture. "It must be hard work—just the three of you. By the way, where did Marc go?"

Jose glances at Louise. She answers, "Oh, no place. Just down to check the tanks, I suppose. You know, to be sure the air-filtration system is working."

"I could use a walk. Can I see the tanks?" you ask.

Jose nods. "Why not? Follow me," he says, rising.

If you follow Jose, turn to page 84.

If you sense danger and decide to use delaying tactics, turn to page 104.

"What are my chances for recovery?"

Silence. Followed by low talk. Then:

"We don't know, Commander. The droid has extensive medical knowledge in its memory banks. It is the best source."

The droid moves closer to you and peers down through its light sensors. Then it speaks in its synthesized, singsong voice. Gone are the "it's a nice day" repeats.

"Commander, analysis of all available data on you, your vital signs, and your injury profile indicates you should not be alive at this time. But . . ."

There is a hesitation: you wait tensely for the droid to speak.

"But what?" you ask.

Flppto speaks.

"You are the *but*, Commander. You are alive! You are in control of your life forces. You are making it through the dark space. It's up to you. Leave the rest to us. The war against the Evil Power Master is *our* job now. You must heal. It's in *your* hands, it's in *your* mind, it's in *you!*"

"But what about the SOS? Those people need help."

"Don't worry, we will take care of that. Rest and heal."

Turn to page 88.

"Never! I'll never surrender. You'll kill us both anyway."

You give the scaly arm one final twist and push the wounded creature away from you, adding a well-placed kick as a final insult.

Then you drop into a crouch and begin to advance on the creature that holds Tara. Tara has come prepared. While the creature is watching you, she slowly and stealthily withdraws a slender, flexible stiletto from the belt around her waist. With a sudden, jabbing move, she sinks the stiletto into the thigh of the creature. You leap upon him, wrestle him to the ground, and deliver a paralyzing blow to the base of his skull.

"Well done, Tara. I'm glad you were with me," you say, catching your breath.

"Not so bad yourself," she responds, grinning.

You take the prisoners back to base for interrogation. A small dose of truth serum is enough—they divulge the name and location of the main base of the Evil Power Master. You send an attack force to a small planet nearby. The force successfully destroys the Evil Power Master's base, but not without a fight—half of your forces are lost in the battle. But, for now at least, the Lacoonian System is safe.

The End

"Okay, Flppto, we can't waste time around here now. You're coming with me. I beg you to forgive me." You rouse the Martian.

He nods and allows you to half-carry, half-drag him to your transporter, just beyond the perimeter of the research facility.

"Fine friend you are. What a reception," Flppto mumbles. You nod, feeling sad and guilty. Then Flppto lapses into semiconsciousness.

Several times during the trip back to headquarters, Flppto gains complete consciousness. He apologizes for sneaking up on you. And he forgives you for the wound.

Meanwhile you have been in contact with Tara, assigning to her prime responsibility for surveillance of the Pwasonn Research Facility. Within a short time, aerial reconnaissance, using advanced equipment, is hovering over Pwasonn. The life-sensing machines and the energy-source measurement devices aboard show maximum negative readings from the facility; it's clearly a base for the Evil Power Master. But the reconnaissance crews have made too much noise. The Evil Power Master is alerted and escapes to continue his infamous career.

The End

Out into the night you go, staying close to the sides of buildings, in the shadows. The very fact that you are sneaking around is enough to get you in trouble. But it is your decision to play it as though your cover has already been stripped away.

There seems to be some activity over by the fish tanks. You head in that direction, using whatever scant cover there is.

Whap! You bump into a ventilator partially hidden by weeds. The opening is quite large—a person could fit into it. Voices are coming from inside the ventilator. Straining, you can just make out the words: "We will never capitulate . . . never . . . time will be . . ." It is Tara's voice!

This is it—a base for the Evil Power Master! The grate over the ventilator shaft lifts off easily. Odd that they didn't station guards around this place at all. But then, who could believe the Evil Power Master would be based on any planet—particularly Lacoos?

Down you go. It's hot, cramped, dark, and unpleasant in the shaft. It takes you a long time to worm your way through the shaft. Finally you reach a grating in a wall and look down on a huge, square, concrete chamber. The room is loaded with computers! They are manned by a team of slave droids all painted a brilliant orange. A blue insignia shaped like a four-headed dragon has been painted on each droid, at the spot where its face should be.

Go on to the next page.

In the center of the room stands Marc. He begins to pace back and forth, glancing nervously at the computers, checking his watch. He glances at Jose and Louise, who sit at a special command module.

For more than an hour you peer down, won-

dering what will come next. Finally one of the droids prepares a tape for broadcast. Marc orders it played over the communication grid.

Turn to page 87.

"Flppto! Flppto! Come in! It's me. Over."

Minutes pass. You repeat the message over your communicator, hoping that no one around here is monitoring airwaves. Finally there is a response.

"Flppto here. What's up, Commander?"

"I need you, and fast. I'm onto something. What's going on back there?"

"Lots of arguments. No agreements. Time is running out. Where are you, Commander?"

You give him your coordinates, tell him precisely where to meet you on the perimeter of the research facility, and sign off to wait for his arrival. Tara did not respond to your call. You hope that Flppto can warn her.

Hours pass slowly. His approach has to be quiet, and he'll have to use the same type of slow transporter you did—travel at hyperspace speeds is too risky here.

You hug the ground at the perimeter of the facility, waiting in the half-light for Flppto's arrival. Finally you are aware of movement to your right. At first you think it is a light breeze blowing up from the sea, causing movement in the vegetation. Then you think it must be an animal rustling in the bushes. Finally you decide it's Flppto. But no recognition code is given.

What now? Is it Flppto, or is it the enemy?

*If you decide to fire at the noise,
turn to page 107.*

*If you decide to remain quiet, hoping it's
Flppto, turn to page 101.*

Despite the urgency of the situation, you know that the Congress must be informed. You approach the leaders. Tara has reached them first and is already deep in conversation. She is trying to persuade them to order a full strike. It's a calculated risk to order a full strike. There is danger of a devastation so complete that it can destroy the entire system by shock waves and deadly fallout. But the Evil Power Master represents an eternal danger to the system. Perhaps the risk is worth it.

The Congress leaders decide—full strike it is. The combat crews are mounted. The weapons are trained on the target. The commands are given. The Lacoonians fire.

With no chance to escape the blast, the Evil Power Master's followers return fire. And in the gigantic explosions that occur, all life forms in the system suffer. In minutes, sixty percent have died. The lucky sixty percent. The others linger on in pain.

But the Evil Power Master is victorious. His nature is more negative, more destructive, than the powers of weapons. He is not damaged by the blasts. He reigns supreme—and alone—in the universe.

The End

"Lead the way, Jose," you say, trying to sound casual. You hope that you have made the right choice.

You haven't.

The minute you step outside you are surrounded by six thugs, ex-convicts from the planet Mandor in the Zaross System. You've seen these thugs before on an earlier mission. They are killers. Well over seven feet tall, they have brawny arms covered with hair as coarse as steel wool. But their size is less terrifying than their smell—it is the smell of death.

You make a last, desperate dash for freedom. But they simply laugh and pick you up like a harmless kitten. In a viselike grip, one thug carries you to a windowless room. A metal door slams closed and you hear a key click in the lock. For you, the war against the Evil Power Master is over.

The End

You decide that Flppto is right. The problem is just too big. You shouldn't fly off the handle and go chasing out into space on your own. It is definitely better to seek the advice and concurrence of the Congress, where older and, you hope, wiser heads can provide good guidance.

You find Tara, and she leads the way through the throngs in the Great Hall. The two of you speak earnestly as leaders listen attentively. They examine the printouts and spend time in earnest conference. Finally they reach a decision. The eldest speaks.

"*Attack Follop*—that is the main thrust. The secondary activity will be rounding up the eleven other bases. You and Tara will accompany the main attack force. Flppto will go with the others."

Through the next thirty-eight hours, the battle ebbs and flows. Spaceships, delta fighters, and supply transports explode with brilliant flashes of orange and white. Still more attackers continue to surge forward. Three planets fall to the will of the Evil Power Master. As they die they leave no trace but a murmur of anguish.

Turn to page 112.

"TIME IS UP. THREE DAYS ARE OVER. TOO LATE."

Marc signals to Jose and Louise. They hit buttons on the command module, activating a massive laser beam. Somewhere in the multigalactic Lacoonian System another planet is coming apart, its life forms destroyed.

"So simple," you think. "Marc is the head of this group. He looks human, but it's the Evil Power Master in another of his disguises."

You shift your position slightly to relieve the cramps in your legs. It's a mistake. The noise you make is immediately picked up by the two droids who function as security police. They alert the others.

The two droids have you in their grip. Marc advances, no longer the kind host of the dinner table. He grins a vicious grin. Helpless, you will now and forever be a witness to the power of true evil.

The End

The weeks pass by in a confusion of pain and sleep and more pain, followed, eventually, by periods of well-being and peace. You concentrate your energy on healing. You follow the diet, the prescribed course of medicines, and exercise.

While you are working your way back to health, Tonto and Flppto successfully rescue the party that sent the SOS. Then the mission returns to base, where you can receive proper care.

Back at Lacoos, the doctors and hospital staff encourage you and are pleased with your progress toward full recovery. But it is not easy, not easy at all. For now, the struggle against the Evil Power Master must go on without you—until you are well enough to lead the Rapid Force again.

The End

"No time, Flppto, no time for chat. I need you. Let's go."

You dash from the Central Computer Service to your ship in no time flat.

The blast-off, the leap into hyperspace, and the journey to Follop take less time than you thought. Then, just on the perimeter of Follop's atmosphere, you run into trouble. Your ship is attacked by planetary defenders. But you keep on going.

Suddenly you see it: a light track—broad, golden, shining—flows away from Follop, straight toward the Void of Niro.

If you follow the light track to the Void, thinking it is an escape beam for the Evil Power Master, turn to page 109.

If you ignore the light track and go on into Follop, turn to page 110.

"I don't like to do this, but we'll take arms with us. It's a hostile move, but we don't know what's going on out there."

The two of you strap on laser blasters and cautiously leave the capsule. But before you have a chance to use your weapons, a force field surrounds you, locking you into immobility. You feel your energy draining away. Your arms hang by your sides like lead weights. Your laser blasters are useless.

Flppto says, "Sorry, Commander, I was wrong. I got us into this."

"That's okay, Flppto. I agreed. It was worth a try."

Then, as suddenly as the force field grasped you, it releases you.

Turn to page 93.

"I'll never join you." You grit your teeth in determination. The temptation to live—in any fashion—is strong. But your will is stronger. You have been tested before; you will not relent. "Never!" you shout.

"I THOUGHT SO. WELL, SO BE IT. FOOLISH LACOONIAN—OFFERED THE COSMOS, YOU CHOOSE DEATH. THERE'LL BE OTHERS SMARTER THAN YOU."

An intense pain binds you in its deadly grasp, and that is all you ever know.

The End

"Commander, I suggest caution."

"Thanks, Flppto, but we have to take this chance. The fate of the System could depend on our courage."

The droid nods in agreement and begins to arm the ship's defensive weapons.

"No, they won't be any good to us," you say. "Show openness, show good will."

The droid nods. Then the space vehicle is inside the white-lighted space. Seconds later you are surrounded by humanoid figures dressed in light-colored robes. They are not armed. A group of four seems to be a welcoming party.

The droid pushes forward, seemingly anxious to leave the capsule. "Pushy droid," you think. It speaks.

"Iamheretakemenowmyprayershavebeenanswered."

The droid leaps from the hatch and lands on the metallic hangar deck with a clanging thud. Immediately the droid is surrounded, set upright, and led away. You hear its voice . . .

"Hoorayhoorayhoorayhooray . . ."

"Flppto, what's going on? What happened with that droid?"

"Maybe we'd better use the weapons, Commander," says Flppto. "This looks strange. No one's talking out there."

*If you decide to arm yourselves,
turn to page 90.*

*If you hold firm to your peaceful approach,
turn to page 58.*

Now a robot appears, hovering in the air above you. It's Rendoxoll—the most intelligent non-life creation in the universe, and a hero of the Lacoonian System.

"Welcome. Have no fear—I will not harm you," Rendoxoll says.

"What are you doing here?" you ask.

"Searching for our mutual enemy, as you are. I can use good people like you. Join me."

So, you, Flppto, and the droid join forces with Rendoxoll. Your band has talent and great will. Only time will tell if you can defeat the Evil Power Master.

The End

"Full reverse! Full reverse!"

"Right! I'm trying!"

"Try harder!"

It's too late. You are swept into the giant structure, into the region of the white light in a powerful tractor beam. Inside, nothing moves. Nothing happens. Slowly your life functions slow down. Your breath rate drops from 30 per minute to 20, to 10, to 1, and then to ½. Your pulse drops from its normal 50 (already low at the start) to 25, then to 3 beats per minute. Your mind is clear, clearer than ever before. You know that you are suspended in time and space, unable to struggle.

Suddenly a creature appears before your eyes. It is Rendoxoll, fabled robot hero of the Lacoonian System, an artificial intelligence without equal. You had thought it was destroyed! It peers into your spaceship. It speaks: "Lucky for you I recognized you, Commander. Otherwise, you and your crew would have been disintegrated. We're careful about strangers out here. Have to be—too dangerous not to be."

Gradually, you feel your strength returning. Flppto wiggles the place where his ears would be, if he had ears. The droid swivels, then seems to sigh. You take a deep breath. "You had us scared, Rendoxoll. That was close!"

Turn to page 97.

"Looks bad, Flppto. Prepare to blast our way out."

Flppto hesitates. "If you are certain, Commander. But perhaps we should analyze the situation more closely."

But you know trouble when you see it. This could be the home base of the Evil Power Master.

"Prepare, lock, and fire," you command.

Just then a voice—unearthly, non-humanoid, non-droid—penetrates your craft.

"I must warn you, Earthling. Get out while you can! The Evil Power Master is loose again."

You recognize the voice: it's Rendoxoll, the brightest specimen of artificial intelligence in the universe. Rendoxoll is a hero of legend, and its desire to quell the Evil Power Master is as strong as your own. You thought that Rendoxoll had perished in that conflict, but it has survived to join forces in your struggle yet again.

"I held the Evil Power Master prisoner in my secret base here. But he escaped in his true magical state. There are no pilots on those delta fighters—it is his power alone, the power of evil, guiding them. Escape, I tell you; escape!"

The transmission ends, and you look up to see a delta fighter approaching in firing position.

Outside your ship the Evil Power Master's fleet is advancing. The delta fighters fire, and you are vaporized in a flash of orange. The Evil Power Master has triumphed. Perhaps, however, Rendoxoll has made it to safety and will return to fight against the Evil Power Master.

The End

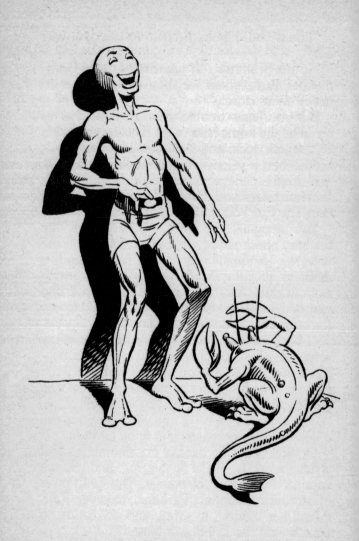

"Well, as long as you are here, welcome aboard," says Rendoxoll. "And come see the Evil Power Master himself. He's powerless now—we captured him using bribery and treachery. His favorite tools became ours. His followers were all too eager to sell him for a price."

Rendoxoll leads you to a cell. There, huddled in the corner, is a soft, squishy creature. He cowers, harmless. The Evil Power Master reminds you of a lobster out of its shell.

To your surprise, Flppto laughs.

The End

You allow your ship to be escorted to the hangar of the green hexagon. Once inside, a hideous laugh fills the cavern, and in a puff of acrid smoke, the figure of a human materializes. . . . The figure is two-sided! There are two faces, one young, the other old. The figure points to a pile of scorched metal and a heap of circuits and transistors. It is all that remains of what once must have been an intelligent non-living form. Flppto points at the heap on the floor. He speaks.

"It's Rendoxoll, the great Rendoxoll—the hero of the Lacoonian System." There is a quaver in his voice.

"You are so right, so right; even *it* could not defeat me, for all its intelligence." The Evil Power Master cackles and smiles. Then, turning, he leads you to a second cavernlike area. There heaps upon heaps of droids lie, smashed and scorched and ruined.

"There must be thousands of droids," you say to Flppto. You glance at your droid's impassive sensors—it does not make a sound.

Then you look in the far corner at piles of bones and skulls. Humans have met the same fate as droids here. The sound of the door clanging shut behind you interrupts your terrible thoughts. And you know that you have been locked in this cavernous room to perish.

The End

Flppto leaves the space vehicle with the droid, on an expedition to try to locate the people who sent the SOS. You are barely aware of what is going on. Getting well is the main thing in your mind. Slowly, you do mend.

Communications from the base hospital on Lacoos enable your healing to be guided by the very best medical personnel in the multigalactic System.

Weeks later, Flppto and Tonto rejoin you. They have rescued the crew that sent the SOS and all are now safely aboard. You are well enough to join them in a discussion about the Evil Power Master and the strange occurrences in the galactic system. He has been very busy in his selective destruction of small, isolated planets in remote sectors.

Inactivity has left you frustrated and angry. Your world is embattled. The war against the Evil Power Master continues, a war with no clearly defined lines. Your ever-changing enemy appears in different forms, both human and animal. He is cloudlike energy one minute, and a hideous jellylike mass the next. But he has a genius for destruction. And you are out of action. You know that you'll get better, but it's hard to be patient.

The End

It could be Flppto, you think. But you hunker down even closer to the earth. You wait. The rustling stops. The light ocean breeze abates.

No Flppto. No enemy. Just you.

"Where is he?" you ask yourself.

But there is no answer. Maybe he's been captured, you think.

Just then you see some activity down at the group of buildings. Doors open and floodlights switch on, bathing the area in an eerie, white-blue glare.

Out of the sky a flight of deltas dashes in, hovering for a few moments, then landing in tight, orderly precision on a large field.

You stare with horrified fascination as a bizarre assortment of creatures disembarks from the deltas. Some are shaped like humans with extra-large heads, arms, and legs. But others look like mere shadows, with light areas where eyes and mouths should be. Still others are reptilian.

There is a tap on your shoulder.

Turn to page 108.

You try to make Flppto comfortable. But while you are bandaging his wounds, a paralyzing vapor surrounds you. Moments later you and Flppto are carried away, prisoners of the Evil Power Master.

You are imprisoned in empty fish tanks, the glass of which is too thick to break.

A day later, the Evil Power Master pays you a visit. He taunts you, saying, "Lacoonian, give up. It's easy. Don't fight me anymore. Join me!" He laughs. "You'll see. In time, you will see."

You are firm, and so is Flppto. You will never join him, never. The mockery in the Evil Power Master's voice makes you angry. "Never!" you cry. You look at Flppto. He is calm, but grave.

"Nor shall I join you," he says. An understanding passes between you and your Martian friend. Flppto does not share your anger—his resolve to fight the Evil Power Master is based on logic. But you and Flppto are of the same mind—ready to endure anything rather than give in.

The End

"Great," you say. "Give me one second, Jose—I'd like to use the washroom. I'll be right back."

You go into the washroom and open the window above the sink. You boost yourself up to the ledge and drop with a thud to the ground, scraping your knee painfully against the side of the building.

You have to hurry. They'll be on to you at any time now. And if these really are the Evil Power Master's people, they'll play for keeps.

Inside, the door bursts open. You see Louise and Jose silhouetted against the light of the room. Jose has a laser pistol in his hand.

"Stop! Stop where you are! There is no escape," he calls out from the window.

You are sure that they haven't really seen you yet. You freeze against the side of the building, waiting to make a quick break.

Jose turns to search the other side of the building. In a flash, you are running faster than you have ever run in your life. You zig and zag in an attempt to confuse them.

Go on to the next page.

The laser shots zap against rock and earth, causing little chips to ricochet in all directions. A burst of chipped rock hits you on the side of the face, but you keep on going. You don't dare look back.

You reach the dock, panting and gasping. A small jet-powered boat is tied to one of the pilings.

If you try to escape in the boat, turn to page 111.

If you hide under the dock, turn to page 118.

You turn and fire your laser pistol. The beam stabs the darkness and finds its mark: Flppto, the Martian, tumbles forward, grasping his arm. His face is contorted with pain.

You grab your wounded friend. He regards you calmly, knowing the reason for your error.

A quick examination shows that the damage is serious but probably not life-threatening. Flppto sinks to the ground, unconscious.

If you decide to get Flppto back to headquarters to get medical attention right away, turn to page 78.

If you decide to give him first aid and continue the search for the Evil Power Master, turn to page 102.

108

Spinning around, you expect to face a hostile guard. It's Flppto.

"Thank goodness you're here, Flppto."

"Wouldn't dream of missing it."

You and Flppto watch in dismay as the crews from the deltas gather in formation. They stand at rigid attention. Marc steps to the front and slowly peels off his human form. All that remains is a bright, golden light about the size of a grapefruit. The delta crews sink to their knees and bow their heads, their hands clasped before this strange power.

The crowd sends up a chant: "Oh, great and glorious Evil Power Master, we bow to you."

Jose and Louise stand next to the glowing energy; they are sentinels, disciples of this force.

There is a sharp noise, then nothing. Only a murmuring sound is left, to echo for all time in all places. The main planet of the Lacoonian System disintegrates. The Evil Power Master has triumphed again.

The End

You choose to follow the light track into the Void on the chance that it is either the escape route of the Evil Power Master or the route to his base.

But the Evil Power Master has counted on your curiosity and determination. The beam of light is a trick—and it has terrible powers. Your skin begins to wrinkle; your muscles lose their size and shape. Your hair thins. Your teeth rattle in your mouth. You are dying of instant old age. The Evil Power Master's last laugh is on you.

The End

"We're going into Follop, Flppto. Haven't got time to waste now."

The Follop defenses suddenly, mysteriously cease. Your ship cruises in unopposed, landing near a large city.

A strange—perhaps magical—force overcomes you and Flppto. You seem to drift on a cushion of air. Everything seems beautiful, comfortable, and right. Horror is gone; agony does not exist.

A voice floats toward you.

"NOT SO EVIL AFTER ALL, IS IT? WHY NOT JOIN US?"

Your thoughts drift, examining the question and the choice. Battles and fighting are forgotten.

What will you decide? How can you know that the creature you call the Evil Power Master is *really* evil? Maybe you can't know. Maybe he isn't.

The End

The jet engine in the old boat bursts into life at the touch of the starter. You barely have time to cast off. But you escape your pursuers, who now total at least a dozen.

You pull out the throttle, and the boat leaps away. You hurtle across the water, bound for a harbor in a nearby city. Through the night's mist, the city lights grow brighter. In an hour you are safely docked, and you check in at a Rapid Force base.

Then you return to headquarters and report your findings. The Congress sends out an expeditionary force, under your leadership, to Pwasonn. Your command ship circles the area, directing the assault forces. In fierce fighting that lasts almost three hours, the Pwasonn Facility is taken. But the Evil Power Master escapes. His power is weakened, but only for the time being. The Lacoonian System will remain secure only until the Evil Power Master regains his full strength.

The End

You push on. More waves of assault ships are beaten back. Tara is once again a formidable fighter, leading the attack and encouraging her warriors. Together you survive many onslaughts by the Evil Power Master's followers.

With one last massive effort, you and Tara break through Follop's defensive shield with six other ships. You are rocked by the entry into the force field. Your ship turns a bright red from the

heat of the entry. You line up your sights on the headquarters of the Evil Power Master. Then you fire.

Wham! The building disintegrates. The base of the Evil Power Master is no more.

Peace reigns. Tara gives you a thumbs-up sign. The multigalactic Lacoonian System lives on.

The End

There is no time to waste. Good old Flppto, you think. He's always on top of things. What a Martian!

The dash to the hangars is difficult because of the anxious crowds. But finally you make it. Your ship is ready for immediate use.

"Check accelerator levels, Flppto."

"Check."

"Energizer levels."

"Check."

Go on to the next page.

"Gyrostabilizers."

"Check."

"Let's go."

You and Flppto zoom into space. There has been no time to alert the others. Your hands are full with the mission before you.

Soon you break through the protecting radiation belt. Your ship is showered with small meteorites and space debris. A fair-sized meteorite hits you, and the ship rocks. But all systems register normal after Flppto manipulates the autorepair cycles.

"Coming up on the satellite, Commander."

"Right, Flppto. Watch their deltas. They are *fast.*"

"No problem for an old Martian like me, Commander."

Three waves of deltas hit you, but each time Flppto beats them off with a devastating array of shots. Finally you are zeroed in on the base of the Evil Power Master.

"Yield or we'll fire," you command over the communication system.

The satellite bristles with an array of antennas. They must be part of the laser-cannon positioning device that pinpoints the planets for destruction.

"NEVER. I'LL NEVER YIELD, FOOL."

You don't hesitate. One massive blast of your laser eradicates the Evil Power Master's base. The light from the explosion illuminates the heavens, and a cry penetrates the universe: "FOOL! YOU WILL BE SORRRYYYY!"

The End

Colin describes what's been happening and why he believes it's the base of the Evil Power Master.

"At first I thought it was just illness taking the men. Now I'm convinced otherwise. Everything—people, machines, *everything*—breaks down. First there's an eerie silence, then the breakdowns, then ghostly murmurings. It's got to be the Evil Power Master—it's just got to be. It's like what he did to the people on Earth, years ago."

As Colin finishes speaking, a maniacal voice fills the air.

"RIGHT YOU ARE! NOW IT'S *YOUR* TURN! IT'S ALL OVER FOR YOU, FOR ALL OF YOU. LONG LIVE EVIL!"

The End

The old wooden dock offers little protection. Footsteps thud overhead, and you soon find yourself looking up into the menacing eyes of Marc. He and Jose lead you away to imprison you in the storage room of the Pwasonn Facility.

When news of your defeat reaches the Congress, the will of the Lacoonians to survive as free life forms seems to die. The Evil Power Master terrorizes the System, forcing his demands, until all of the planets capitulate. The Evil Power Master rules supreme.

You are long since dead. But a pile of old, musty bones in a forgotten research facility still tells the tale of one who fought in vain against the Evil Power Master.

The End

ABOUT THE AUTHOR

R.A. MONTGOMERY is an educator and publisher. A graduate of Williams College, he also studied in graduate programs at Yale University and New York University. After serving in a variety of administrative capacities at Williston Academy and Columbia University, he co-founded the Waitsfield Summer School in 1965. Following that, Montgomery helped found a research and development firm specializing in the development of educational programs. He worked for several years as a consultant to the Peace Corps in Washington, D.C. and West Africa. He is now both a writer and a publisher.

ABOUT THE ILLUSTRATOR

PAUL ABRAMS has worked as an artist for Marvel Comics and *Heavy Metal* magazine. He has also taught art professionally and, in addition, was a rock musician for several years. Mr. Abrams lives in New Paltz, New York.

DO YOU LOVE CHOOSE YOUR OWN ADVENTURE®?

**Let your younger brothers and sisters
in on the fun.**

You know how great CHOOSE YOUR OWN ADVEN-
TURE® books are to read and reread. But did you
know that there are CHOOSE YOUR OWN ADVEN-
TURE® books for younger kids too? They're just as
thrilling as the CHOOSE YOUR OWN ADVENTURE®
books you read and they're filled with the same kinds
of decisions and different ways for the stories to end—
but they're shorter with more illustrations and come in
a larger, easier-to-read size.

So get your younger brothers and sisters and any-
one else you know between the ages of seven and
nine in on the fun by introducing them to the exciting
world of CHOOSE YOUR OWN ADVENTURE.®
They're on sale wherever Bantam paperbacks are sold.

AV10